Hamish McHaggis

This book belongs to

....

....

This is Hamish the haggis
of the McHaggis clan,
rarely seen by
the eyes of man.

Hamish

Rupert Harold the Third
is an English gent,
travelling far from
his home in Kent.

Rupert

Our Jeannie's an osprey with wide sweeping wings,
who is easily distracted by all sorts of things.

Jeannie

Angus

Young Angus is cheeky and likes playing the fool,
whatever he's doing, he's got to look cool.

For Marcus with love. L.S.

For all my "clan"
with love and thanks. S.J.C.

Text and Illustrations copyright © Linda Strachan and Sally J. Collins

www.hamishmchaggis.co.uk
www.lindastrachan.com

First published in paperback in Great Britain 2009

The rights of Linda Strachan and Sally J. Collins to be identified as
the author and illustrator of this work have been asserted by them in
accordance with the Copyright, Designs and Patents Act 1988

Design – Tony Fleetwood
Printing – Printer Trento, Italy

Published by
GW Publishing
PO Box 6091
Thatcham
Berks
RG19 8XZ.

Tel + 44 (0)1635 268080
www.gwpublishing.com

ISBN 978-0-9561211-2-7

Hamish McHaggis

and
The Clan Gathering

By Linda Strachan
Illustrated by Sally J. Collins

"What's that, Grandpappy?" Hamish stared at the tattered cloth. He sneezed twice and a cloud of dust rose into the air. "It's covered in stoor and it's clarty!"

"Why, it's the McHaggis clan banner, my boy," Rory McHaggis explained. "It's ancient and very, very precious."

"We can't carry that at the Clan Gathering, Grandpappy." Hamish gently shook his head.

CLAN McHAGGIS BANNER

"Aye, lad," Rory grinned. "That's why I've asked each member of the clan to bring a wee square of cloth decorated with something special from their part of the world. It will make a grand new banner."

"Now that's a braw idea!" said Hamish.

Jeannie popped her head through the doorway. "We'll need lots of help to sew all those patches together," she told Rory.

My love is like a red, red rose...

Angus whispered to Rupert. "What's a clan?"

But Rupert had his nose in a book and was muttering to himself.

"*My love is like a red, red rose.*"

What's a clan, Rupert?" Angus asked, again.

"It's like a huge family of all the folk who share the same name," Rupert explained. "The McHaggises live all over the world and lots of them are coming home to Coorie Doon for the Clan Gathering.

"I'm not sure I like the sound of that," Angus said, hugging his tail tightly.

"I'm sure some of them will be shy too, Angus," said Jeannie. "But you can tell them all about Scotland, and Hamish says we are taking them on a tour of some of our favourite places!"

"Do you know," Rupert said, "I am a poet, like Robert Burns, and I'm sure I'm partly Scottish, too. I think *my* great-great-grandfather might have been Scottish.

I'm a poet, don't you know,
like Rabbie Burns from long ago!

Jeannie snorted, but she tried to hide her grin when Rupert looked upset. "You might need to work on that a bit, before you call yourself a poet."

"Harrumph!" Rupert frowned at her over his glasses.

"Who is Robert Burns?" asked Angus.

Rupert showed Angus his book. "He's a very famous Scottish poet."

The next day Rory was very excited. "My old friend, Mary Sue McHaggis, is arriving today from America and she's bringing the wee twins with her."

"Where is America?" asked Angus. "Is it very far away? Have we been there in the Whirry Bang, Hamish?"

"We've not been quite that far in the Whirry Bang, Angus." Hamish laughed. "Not yet, anyway."

"Look, I've made a big map of the world. You can help me stick
wee flags in it to show all the places the McHaggises come from."
"That sounds like fun," said Angus.

It wasn't long before Mary Sue and the twins arrived at the Hoggle.

"Why it's just grand to be here and you look as handsome as ever, Rory!" she said, giving him a big kiss.

Rory blushed quite orange. "Mary Sue! Come and meet my grandson, Hamish," he said quickly.

Mary Sue had a twinkle in her eye. "And a fine McHaggis he is, Rory. Just like his gorgeous Grandpappy!"

She turned to the twins. "Meg, Mac, say 'Hi' to Hamish."

Mary Sue spotted Angus hiding behind the chair. "And who's this?"

"That's my friend, Angus," Hamish told her.

"Hi there, Angus! Could you show the twins around and keep them out of trouble?" she asked.

Angus nodded shyly.

The McHaggis clan started arriving at the Hoggle: Pietro and Maria from Italy; Madeleine and Jean Paul from France; Franco from Spain. McHaggises came from Japan, Canada, Australia and New Zealand, from China, India, Germany and Mexico. In fact, they came from everywhere.

All afternoon, Angus, Meg and Mac were on the look out for the visitors. They made a swing on the signpost with an old rope and some sticks.

"The McHaggis Hoggle is that way," giggled Meg, pointing out the path to the Hoggle.

"Welcome to Coorie Doon!" Angus shouted, as he swung around upside down.

Mac put the squares he had collected from the visitors into his basket. "My turn next," he said, joining in the fun.

When Rupert called the three friends in for their tea no one noticed that all the swinging on the signpost had turned it around, and that it was pointing the wrong way. When the last clan bus arrived the driver followed the sign and took the road leading away from the Hoggle.

As it got dark, Hamish started to worry that some of their visitors still hadn't arrived. "It's late," he told Jeannie.

"Some of the Clan McHaggis from Australia and New Zealand should have been here ages ago. I think we should go and look for them."

"Oh, dearie me," Jeannie fluttered her feathers. "They must have got lost."

"Dinna fash yersel, Jeannie." Hamish patted her wing gently. "We'll find them."

Mary Sue looked confused.

"He just told Jeannie not to worry," Angus explained, feeling rather worried himself.

It was a clear night and the full moon made everything look silvery as Hamish and Jeannie went out to search for the lost bus.

"You take the high road, Hamish and I'll fly down the glen," Jeannie squawked as she flew off.

Hamish set out in the Whirry Bang. When he reached the signpost he realised that it had been turned round, so he followed the moonlit road until he found the missing visitors.

Soon they were all safely back at the Hoggle and Hamish explained what had happened.

"We didn't mean to move the signpost," the twins said together.

"We're very, very sorry," said Angus. "Look! We've made you a clootie dumpling and some raspberry bannocks. They're my favourites!"

Bruce McHaggis winked at them. "No worries, mate! Hey, these bannocks are bonza! Stick another couple on the barbie, Hamish!"

The next day, leading the way in the Whirry Bang, Hamish took the McHaggis clan on a grand tour of some of his favourite places around Scotland.

They set off for **Loch Ness** where Nessie lives. Over the bridge to **Sky**

South to **Alloway**, to the cottage where Robert Burns was born.

Next was **Edinburgh** to see the castle and Greyfriars Bobby.

They went for a ride on the wonderful **Falkirk Wheel**.

here was time for a picnic at **Stirling Castle**.

Off to **Glamis Castle** - to go ghost hunting!

The last stop was **Balmoral**, to see the Royal Palace and their friend Shona the squirrel. Then back home to **Coorie Doon**.

"Jeannie!" whispered Angus. "I think there's something wrong with Rupert."

Jeannie nodded. "You're right. He's been very busy all morning. He was haverin' on about trying to prove something, but when I tried to have a keek at his books he quickly snapped them shut. I think you should speak to him, Hamish."

"What's the matter, Rupert?" Hamish offered Rupert an apple from his basket.

"I can't find any trace of my Scottish ancestors." Rupert looked quite miserable. "I really wanted to belong to a clan, or at least be a little bit Scottish," he said.

"Aah, so that's it," said Hamish. "But you are Rupert Harold the *Third*. That's like having a clan of your own."

"Yes, but it's not a Scottish clan and the Clan Gathering is so much fun."

"But you, Jeannie and Angus are all part of the Gathering. We'd never have organised it without you."

"I suppose so," Rupert mumbled.

"That looks braw," said Rory McHaggis as he handed over the clan crest to be sewn into the banner. Everyone wanted to help sew the last few stitches and when it had been completed, they slid it onto a pole.

"Hamish, Rupert. It's finished!" squawked Jeannie. "Come and help us hold it up."

Rupert and Hamish held up the banner using two strong posts and Jeannie inspected it from above.

"Wait a minute," said Angus. "I want to see something."

"What is it?" asked Jeannie.

"This patch from Canada has an osprey on it, Jeannie, and it looks just like you!"

"That's right, Angus. Mavis McHaggis brought that square. It's my cousin Nigel, and she knows him!"

"Hold it up high so we can all see it," said Rory McHaggis.

Rupert smiled. "It does look very splendid," he said.

Hamish had an extra big smile on his face. He and his grandpappy had planned a surprise for Rupert.

The very next day they all took part in the grand McHaggis Clan Parade and everyone had fun at the Gathering Highland Games.

Hamish tried tossing the caber and Jeannie got out of the way just in time.

There were Welly-Throwing and Hurling-the-Clootie-Dumpling competitions.

There was the great
McHaggis tug o' war.

Rupert played the bagpipes and Angus played his drum, while
Mary Sue McHaggis and Grandpappy Rory
danced the Highland Fling.

Heuch!

Yee Ha!

Everyone had a wonderful time.

As the evening approached the clan gathered on McHaggis Knowe.

"What's happening here?" Rupert asked Jeannie.

"A special ceremony," she said, handing him a tartan sash. "Hamish says you have to put this on."

Angus was smiling at Rupert and the twins were giggling behind their hands.

"Rupert Harold the Third," Rory McHaggis said in a loud voice. "As Clan Chief, I hereby declare that you are now an honorary member of the Clan McHaggis."

He presented Rupert with his own special McHaggis bonnet, with a feather in it.

"That makes you an honorary Scot, Rupert," Hamish grinned. "Now you are part of our clan!"

Rupert was delighted. "Och aye! Now that's braw!" he said, in his best Scottish accent and all the McHaggis clan cheered.

DID YOU KNOW?

Coorie Doon means to nestle or cosy down comfortably.

Blether means to gossip or chatter.

Stoor means dust.

Clarty means dirty.

To keek means to take a peek, or look.

Dinna fash yersel means don't get worked up, or don't worry.

Haverin' means talking nonsense.

Och aye! means Oh yes!

Haggis It is commonly thought that a Haggis has three legs, two long and one short. Hamish thinks this is quite ridiculous!

Angus is a Pine Marten.

Pine Martens eat all sorts of things, including berries and mushrooms.

Young **Hedgehogs** are called hoglets.

Ospreys can fly up to 8 miles to find fish to eat.

A Clootie Dumpling is a fruit pudding boiled in a cloth (cloot).

Robert Burns wrote the song "Auld Lang Syne" which is sung all over the world. He was born in 1759.

Only a **Clan Chief** can wear three feathers in his bonnet.

Hamish McHaggis
and the search for The Loch Ness Monster
978-0-9546701-5-3

Hamish McHaggis
and The Edinburgh Adventure
978-0-9546701-7-7

Hamish McHaggis
and The Skye Surprise
978-0-9546701-8-4

Hamish McHaggis
and The Ghost of Glamis
978-0-9546701-9-1

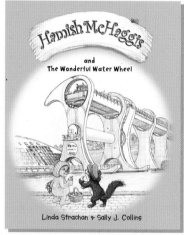

Hamish McHaggis
and the Wonderful Water Wheel
978-0-9551564-0-3

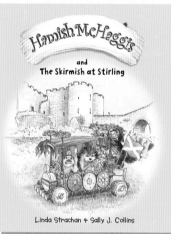

Hamish McHaggis
and the Skirmish at Stirling
978-0-9551564-1-0

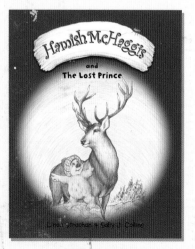

Hamish McHaggis
and The Lost Prince
978-0-9554145-5-8

Hamish McHaggis
Activity and Story Book
978-0-9554145-1-0

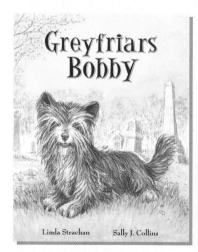

Greyfriars Bobby
978-0-9551564-2-7